To Matthew.
May all your Christmas
wishes come true!

Love.................................

Matthew is **excited**
Christmastime is here!

He says, "I wish for lots and lots of fluffy snow this year!"

Matthew writes to Santa.
The letter takes him ages.

"Perhaps I've wished for way too much?"
(There are over 50 pages!)

Dear Santa,

Matthew decorates the tree
with twinkly lights that glow.

Christmas
decorations

Look at Matthew up on stage.
He's in the Christmas play.

He wished to make
his family proud,
and have the greatest day!

The kitchen's very busy.
Matthew smells
cookies baking.

"I wish that I could eat that bowl of cookie dough Dad's making."

He runs downstairs
to find a pile of
presents beneath
the tree.

This sweater's really itchy.
He tries to grin and bear it,
but Matthew really wishes that
he didn't have to wear it!

Matthew dresses warmly.
His wish for snow came true!

He's off to build a snowman now.
Perhaps he will build two!

Matthew's sledding
down the hill,
"I wish I could
speed up!"

His wish comes true,
his sled is *fast*
when powered by a pup!

It's after Christmas dinner,
and everyone is snoring.
Matthew says to his best friend,
"I wish it was less **BORING!**"

Mom is asking Matthew,
"Did your **BIGGEST** wish come true?"
"Oh yes," he smiles,
"that wish was being..."

"...here with **all** of you!"

Do you wish for fun with friends,
or a family trip that never ends?
Whatever it is that you hold dear,
keep your Christmas wishes here!

I wish...

Published by Put Me In The Story,
a publication of Sourcebooks, Inc.
P.O. Box 4410, Naperville, Illinois 60567-4410
(630) 961-3900
Fax: (630) 961-2168
www.putmeinthestory.com

Date of Production: August 2018
Run Number: HTW_PO201829
Printed and bound in China (GD)
10 9 8 7 6 5 4 3 2 1

Bestselling books starring your child!
www.putmeinthestory.com